SEPTIMUS BEAN

and

HIS AMAZING MACHINE

by Janet Quin-Harkin

pictures by Art Cumings

Parents Magazine Press • New York

To my parents
— J. Q.-H.

Text copyright © 1979 by Janet Quin-Harkin.
Illustrations copyright © 1979 by Art Cumings.
All rights reserved. Printed in the United States of America.
10 9 8 7 6 5 4 3 2 1

Library of Congress Cataloging in Publication Data
Quin-Harkin, Janet. Septimus Bean and his amazing machine.
SUMMARY: Septimus Bean has built an amazing machine
but its use has yet to be discovered.
[1. Inventions—Fiction.   2. Stories in rhyme]
I. Cumings, Art. II. Title. PZ8.3.Q47Se [E] 79–163
ISBN 0–8193–0999–0   ISBN 0–8193–1000–X lib. bdg.

Back in the days of King Albert the Third,

there arrived at the palace (as maybe you've heard)

a strange-looking man who was both long and lean.

He went by the name of Septimus Bean—

and he came with a strange and amazing machine.

It was terribly long, and incredibly high,
and it seemed (from the ground) to reach up to the sky.
It had wheels. It had bells. It was painted bright blue.
But King Albert asked, "Septimus, what does it DO?"

So Septimus pulled on a huge, heavy switch.

The machine gave a rumble, a choke, and a twitch.

Wheels started to spin, fan belts started to run,

and steam valves shot off with a noise like a gun.

Flags waved in the breeze, all the gears took to churning,

and cog wheels kept turning . . . and turning . . . and turning.

The whole machine shook with a horrible shake.

But the King just asked, "Septimus, what does it MAKE?"

Then Septimus bowed and he answered quite slow:

"I regret, good King Al, that I don't rightly know.

I'm sure it is useful one way or another,

but just what it can do I've yet to discover."

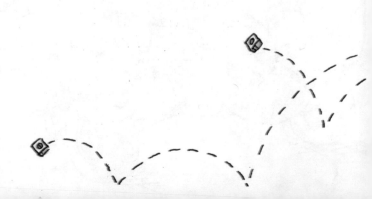

Then in rushed the Queen, Petronella by name,
crying, "Children, see here, what a lovely new game!
What is it, my dear?" she asked of the King.
"We're not really sure WHAT to do with the thing,"
said King Albert the Third. "Its use just is not clear.
Have you any brilliant suggestions, my dear?"

"Perhaps it cleans floors with that long, funny hose
that looks quite a lot like an elephant's nose,"
said the Queen. "It would save us some time on our chores
if we used it instead of a broom to sweep floors."
So the King nodded over to Septimus Bean,
who pulled out the hose and turned on the machine.

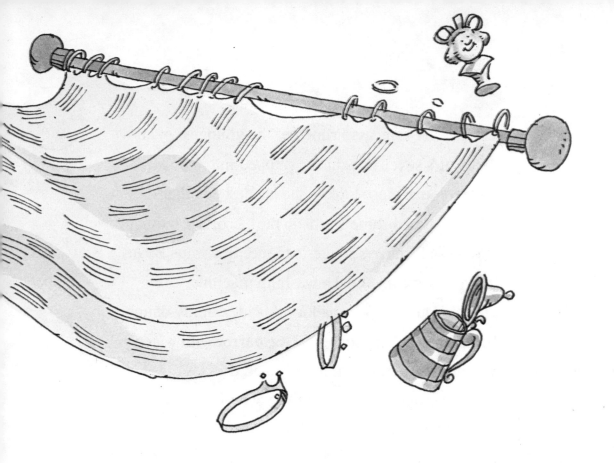

A great blast of air came out with a WHOOSH—
and a tapestry sailed off the wall with a SWOOSH,
sending statues and goblets and coronets flying
and all of the Princesses running off crying.
"Stop! Stop!" cried the Queen as she flew down the room.
"I'd rather sweep floors by myself . . . with a broom!"

Then sweet Princess Primrose, the youngest of all
the King's seven daughters, skipped into the hall.
She took one close look—she needed no other—
and whispered some words in the ear of her mother.
"Princess Primrose suggests to me, Septimus Bean,
that you have invented a washing machine,"
said the Queen. "We shall try this idea of my daughter.
Bring laundry and soap. Fill the barrel with water."
So into the barrel went blouses and dresses
and stockings and skirts of the Seven Princesses.
Then they waited and listened to SQUEAK and to PLOP
till at last the machine slowly ground to a stop.

As she took out the dripping-wet clothing, the Queen
shouted, "Look! The machine worked! The clothes are all clean!"
Until she saw everything happened to shrink
five sizes too small and was spotted with pink.
"Alas, I don't think, Mr. Bean," said the Queen,
"that this is a truly good washing machine."

Then King Albert grinned widely. He had an idea!
He said, "It is becoming increasingly clear
that this thing has a seat and can move its wheels.
Let us drive it a little and see how it feels.
Mr. Bean, take your bright blue invention outside.
It may make a fine coach upon which I can ride.
It might go many miles in a single day
and it will not get tired, and it will not eat hay."
He was all set to start it when up rushed the Queen
crying, "Please leave the driving to Septimus Bean.
Remember, my dear, that you are the King,
and to drive your own coach is just not the royal thing."

So Septimus climbed up, all eager to please.
He pulled on the switch. The machine gave a sneeze
and a snort and a cough and a bang like a gun,
then it shuddered and juddered and started to run.
"It works! Yes, it goes! Yes, it's moving," they cried.
And the Princesses hurriedly stepped to the side
as it rumbled toward them, gathering speed.
"Now stop, Mr. Bean—we have seen all we need,"
cried the King, but in vain. The machine wouldn't slow.
Called the King with alarm, "My, how fast it can go!
Raise the drawbridge at once before poor Mr. Bean
rushes out and away and is never more seen."

Then the drawbridge rose up to slow down the machine
speeding madly along with poor Septimus Bean.
Up went the machine, never slowing at all,
while the people below held their breath for its fall.
But instead it sailed up — and away up it flew,
out over the park as a small speck of blue.

Then the King danced a jig, threw his arms round the Queen,
shouting, "That is the greatest thing I've ever seen!
Who would have guessed that this Septimus Bean
had invented a wonderful flying machine!

Bring my coach, get the horses, send soldiers and bands.
We must honor this man when he finally lands."

Then out went the King and his court to the park
and they waited and searched till it grew almost dark.

"What can have become of our Septimus Bean?
Has he flown off to Africa?" worried the Queen.
Then at last came the news—very sad, very grim—
the machine had been found, but with no trace of him.
They rushed to the scene. What a sad, sorry sight!
There were bits of machine scattered left, scattered right.

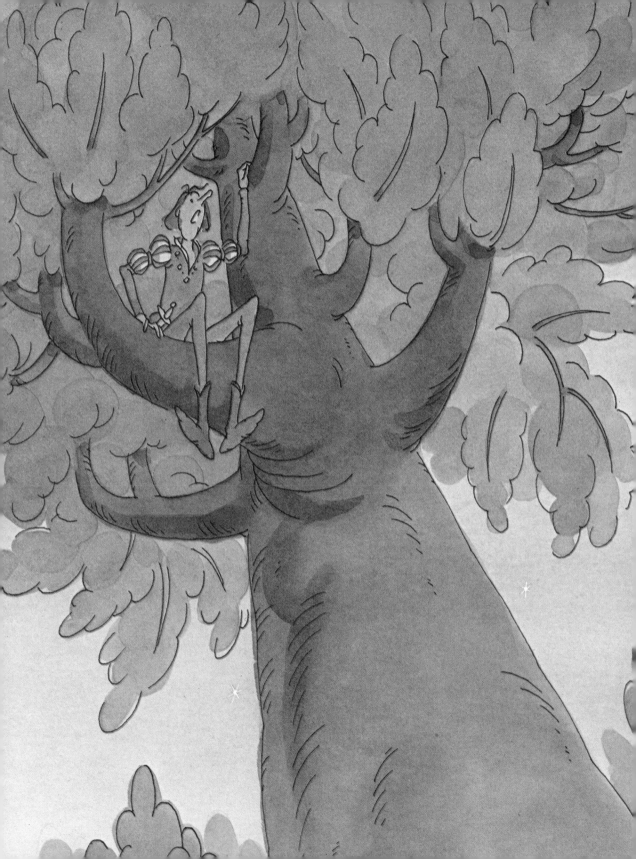

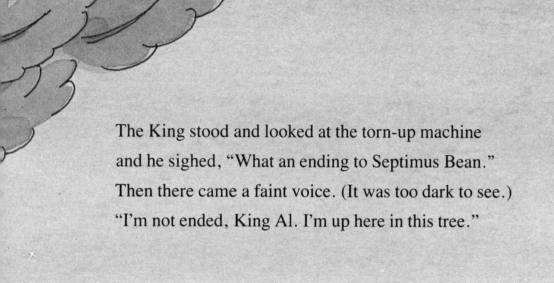

The King stood and looked at the torn-up machine
and he sighed, "What an ending to Septimus Bean."
Then there came a faint voice. (It was too dark to see.)
"I'm not ended, King Al. I'm up here in this tree."

Next morning they went sadly back to the green,

where in twenty-two parts lay the broken machine.

Septimus Bean looked it over, and sighed.

"It's hopeless," he said. And the Princesses cried.

"You'll soon build another, I'm sure," said the Queen.

"You'll fly through the air once more, Septimus Bean."

But Septimus shook his head sadly and said,

"The world must wait. I am going to bed.

I'll never more try to invent a machine.

You can all just forget about Septimus Bean."

But as Septimus turned and walked sadly away,

from behind came the laughter of children at play

and there were the Princesses out on the green

climbing all over the bits of machine.

"Look, Mother. Look, Father," the Princesses cried.

"We can swing, we can climb, we can seesaw and slide."

"Come back, oh, come back," called the King and the Queen.
"You've invented a playground, Septimus Bean.
And what could be nicer to visit every day
than a place you've invented for children to play!"

Then the people were called from each village and town
and the King read a speech that was all written down.
"I name this Bean Park. It's a fine place to play
where each child in my kingdom may come any day.
And we all owe this playground to Septimus Bean,
who flew through the air in a flying machine."

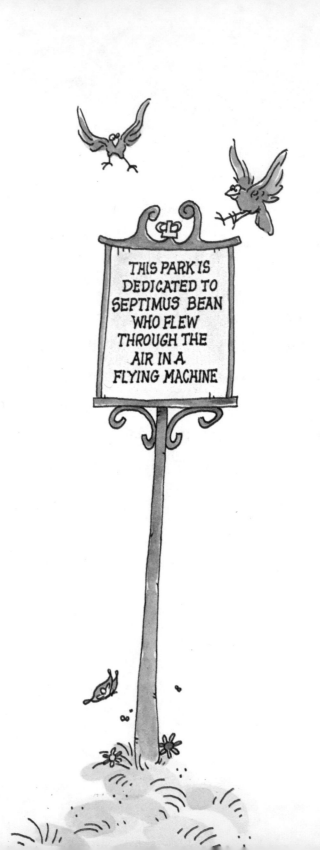

ABOUT THE AUTHOR

JANET QUIN-HARKIN's first children's story, *Peter Penny's Dance,* was judged one of the outstanding books of 1976 by the *New York Times.* And her book *Benjamin's Balloon* was one of PMP's 1979 delights. Although she began to write as a small girl in England, she wanted to become a lion tamer or an opera singer. After her schooling, however, she wrote plays for the British Broadcasting Corporation and then managed a rock group.

It is her background in radio that gives Mrs. Quin-Harkin a great feel for how words sound aside from the way they look on a page. And it is in this spirit that *Septimus Bean* skipped off her pen in Conroe, Texas, where she lives with her husband and their four children.

ABOUT THE ARTIST

"The biggest challenge in illustrating *Septimus Bean,*" says ART CUMINGS, "was designing the machine so that the pieces fit and made it seem almost like a living thing. Luckily, there were great clues in the story to help work it out."

Mr. Cumings has put together Septimus's machine with the same care and skill that he brought to his drawings for other recent children's books: *Please Try to Remember the First of Octember* by Theo. LeSieg (Dr. Seuss), *Charlie's Pets* by Kathryn Ernst, and PMP's own *A Good Fish Dinner* by Barbara K. Walker. A magazine illustrator as well, Mr. Cumings lives with his family in Douglaston, New York.

A